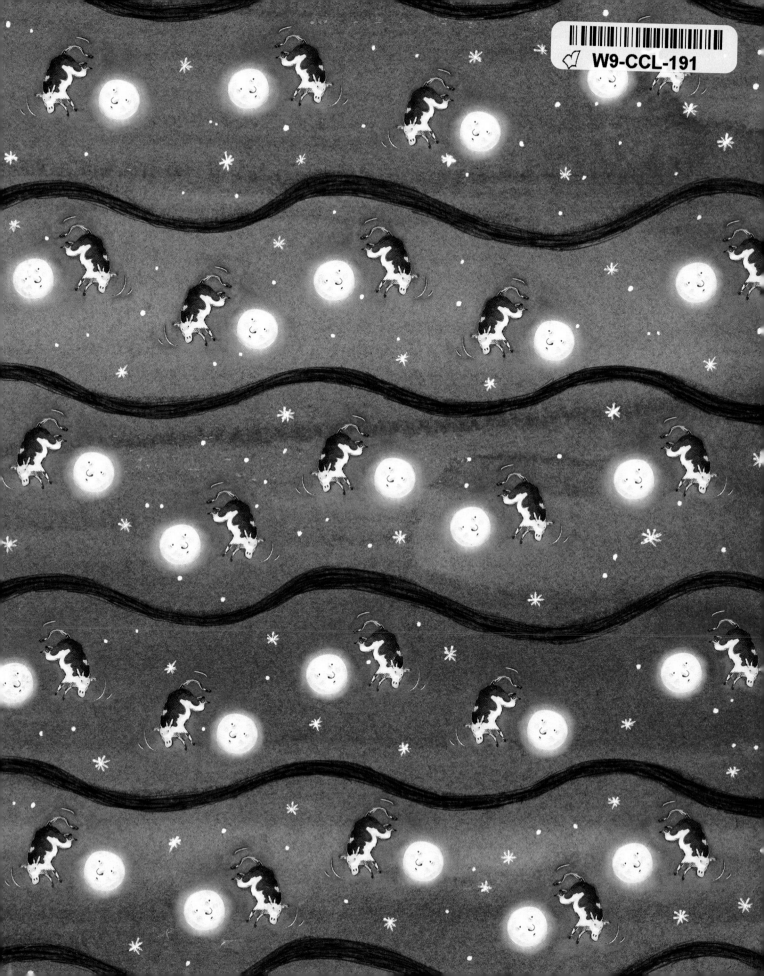

For Kenzie Tarbet Perfett,
who loves cars
J. W.

For Matilda
J. S.

Text copyright © 2015 by Jeanne Willis
Illustrations copyright © 2015 by Joel Stewart

First U.S. edition 2015

Library of Congress Catalog Card Number 2014945704

ISBN 978-0-7636-7402-1

15 16 17 18 19 20 SCP 10 9 8 7 6 5 4 3 2 1

Printed in Humen, Dongguan, China

This book was typset in Adobe Caslon.
The illustrations were done in mixed media.

Candlewick Press
99 Dover Street
Somerville, Massachusetts 02144

visit us at www.candlewick.com

THE COW TRIPPED OVER THE MOON

A Nursery Rhyme Emergency

Jeanne Willis

illustrated by Joel Stewart

CANDLEWICK PRESS

Here comes the ambulance! It's on its way.
Who's had an accident in Storyland today?
Driver, put your foot down. Don't waste time.
This is an Emergency Nursery Rhyme!

Who have we here? It's the farmer's cow!
She fell from a great big height somehow.
"I saw it happen," says a little hound.
"She tripped on the moon and fell to the ground."

She chipped a hoof and grazed her knees!
"Pass me the cow-size bandages, please,"
says the ambulance man to the ambulance crew.
They patch her up, and the cow goes "Moo!"

Here comes the ambulance! Off we go!
It's a Nursery Rhyme Emergency—
anyone we know?
Who's had an accident?
What's wrong now?

Rock-a-Bye Baby fell from a bough.
The wind broke the branch
as she rocked to sleep,
and Baby landed in the compost heap.

"Let's check the patient. Is she hurt?"
No, just covered in weeds and dirt,
with an old banana stuck to her head.
She needs a bath, then straight to bed.

Here comes the ambulance down the lane.
It's a Nursery Rhyme Emergency yet again!
Has Jack Be Nimble burned his bum?
Has Little Jack Horner choked on a plum?

Who could it be, do you suppose?

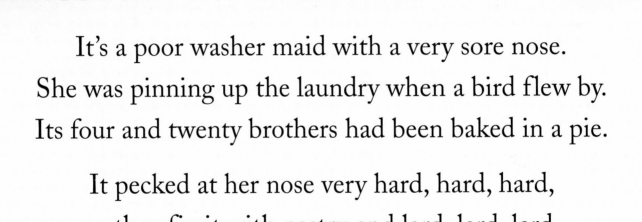

It's a poor washer maid with a very sore nose.
She was pinning up the laundry when a bird flew by.
Its four and twenty brothers had been baked in a pie.

It pecked at her nose very hard, hard, hard,
so they fix it with pastry and lard, lard, lard.

Here comes the ambulance! It's on another call.
It's a Nursery Rhyme Emergency! Someone had a fall.
He fell off the wall. Did he break his leg?

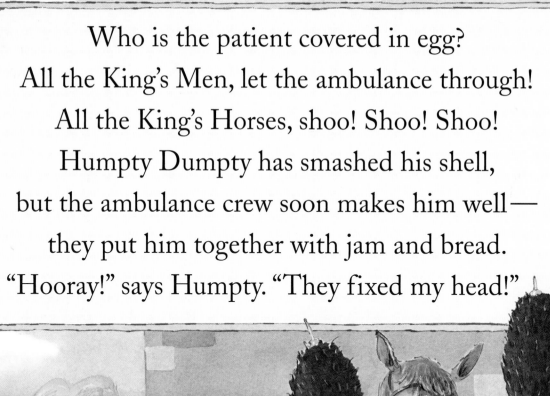

Who is the patient covered in egg?
All the King's Men, let the ambulance through!
All the King's Horses, shoo! Shoo! Shoo!
Humpty Dumpty has smashed his shell,
but the ambulance crew soon makes him well—
they put him together with jam and bread.
"Hooray!" says Humpty. "They fixed my head!"

Here comes the ambulance down the hill.
It's a Nursery Rhyme Emergency—is someone ill?
Someone blew a horn, but we don't know who.
Look beneath the haystack—it's Little Boy Blue!

He was looking after a herd of sheep,
but the tired boy fell fast asleep.
The cows in the corn came and nibbled the hay,
then sat on the stack where the little lad lay.
The crew looks him over: "He isn't in pain,
but he may never play on the horn again—
it's been sat on, flattened, and bent out of shape."
So they fix it with hammers and trumpet tape.

Here comes the ambulance into town.
It's a Nursery Rhyme Emergency—hurry down!
The ambulance arrives and screeches to a stop.
They run to save the weasel . . .

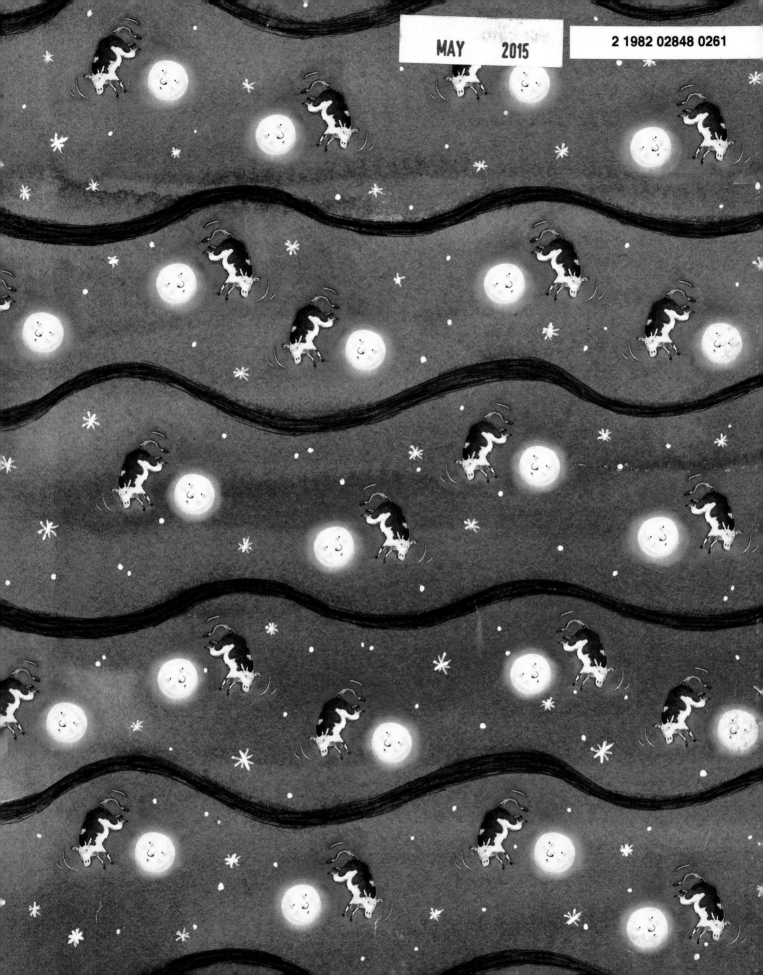